Dr Jekyll and Mr Hyde

by Robert Louis Stevenson

retold by Jenny Alexander

Robert Louis Stevenson (1850–94) grew up in Edinburgh, the son of respectable, middle-class parents. He trained as a lawyer, but by the time he finished university he had decided he would rather be a writer. He said, "fiction is to grown men what play is to the child."

In his early twenties, he developed a serious chest complaint, which was made worse by the cold Scottish climate. He travelled overseas, finally settling in Samoa. His first full-length book was <u>Treasure Island</u> (1883). <u>Dr Jekyll and Mr Hyde</u> was published in 1886; the story came to him in a dream.

Mr Utterson the lawyer was a tall, thin man, who rarely showed any emotion and hardly ever smiled. He did not make friends easily, preferring the company of his family or people he had known since his school days. It didn't seem to matter to him that they had hardly anything in common. For example, what could the dull and dusty lawyer have in common with Mr Richard Enfield, his distant cousin, the dapper man-about-town? Yet every Sunday the two men went out for a walk together.

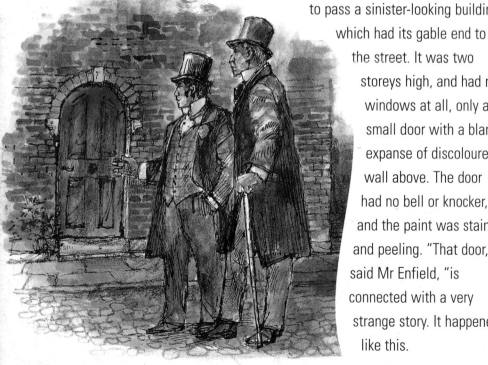

On one such occasion, they happened to pass a sinister-looking building which had its gable end to the street. It was two storeys high, and had no windows at all, only a small door with a blank expanse of discoloured wall above. The door had no bell or knocker, and the paint was stained and peeling. "That door," said Mr Enfield, "is connected with a very strange story. It happened like this.

"I was walking home late one night, when a girl of about eight or nine came running out of a side street and crashed straight into a man who was walking past the corner. It was a simple accident, but to my surprise and horror the man, instead of helping the child up, turned and stamped on her as she lay on the ground. I shouted at him and he tried to run away, but I grabbed him and brought him back. A huddle of angry people had gathered around the girl, who was still lying on the ground.

"I thought the crowd was going to give the man a beating, so I suggested it might be a better idea to make him pay the girl some compensation. A figure of £100 was agreed, and the man brought us here to this door. He unlocked it, went inside, and reappeared some moments later with £10 in cash and a cheque for the other £90. The cheque was not signed by himself, but by a gentleman we both know well. I asked myself, 'Why should a fine, upstanding member of the community want to pay the debts of such a scoundrel?' The only thing I could think of was that the wretch had some kind of hold over him; perhaps he could be blackmailing him about some error in his youth."

Mr Utterson wanted to know who had written the cheque, but Enfield would not tell him. He did not want to endanger the reputation of a good man by indulging in gossip. However, he felt no obligation at all to protect the identity of the wrong-doer, whose name, he freely told his cousin, was Mr Edward Hyde.

Mr Utterson went home with a heavy heart. He had heard the name Edward Hyde before, and he thought he could guess who had written the cheque for him. He looked through his private papers, and took out the will of his old friend, Dr Henry Jekyll. "In the event of my death or disappearance," it said, "I desire all my worldly wealth to go to my friend, Mr Edward Hyde." When Mr Utterson had first seen the will he was worried because he didn't know anything about Mr Hyde. But now he felt even worse because he knew the man was a villain.

Mr Utterson wanted to help his old friend. Whatever hold Mr Hyde had over him, Jekyll was far too gentle and mild-mannered to be able to deal with it himself. So Utterson decided to go to see Mr Hyde and have it out with him. "If he be Mr Hyde," he said to himself, "I shall be Mr Seek."

For several days there was no sign of Mr Hyde at the windowless house.
Utterson lingered nearby, waiting for Mr Hyde, but he never came. Then one
frosty night, he heard a strange, light footfall, and he somehow knew
without looking that it was Mr Hyde. He sank back into the shadows. He
saw a small person cross the road to the shabby door and take his key out
of his pocket. Utterson stepped forward and touched the man's arm.

The man recoiled in alarm. He was very short and slight, and his clothes were several sizes too big for him. "Mr Hyde, I think?" said Utterson. The other man spoke to him with a sort of sneering defiance, although he did not look him in the eye. "That is my name," he said. "What do you want?"

Mr Utterson was overcome by a sudden feeling of deep disgust towards the man, a feeling which seemed out of proportion even to the weasly look of him, his ugly rasping voice and the repugnant deed he had done. Utterson made a huge effort to stand his ground, and remain polite. "I am a friend of Dr Jekyll," he said. "And as we have bumped into each other like this, right here at your front door, I thought perhaps you might like to ask me in." Mr Hyde laughed in his face. Then he went into the house and shut the door without another word.

Now there was nothing for it; if Mr Hyde would not speak to him,
Utterson would just have to talk to Dr Jekyll. He would make the doctor tell
him what was going on. He went straight to Jekyll's house. The door was
opened by Jekyll's butler, Poole, who told Utterson his master was not at
home. Utterson asked Poole whether he was acquainted with Mr Hyde.
Poole told him Mr Hyde was often at the house; he had his own key, in fact,
and the servants had orders to obey him.

"But I have never met him here," said Utterson.

"He doesn't dine with the doctor, sir. He mostly uses the laboratory door
at the back of the house in his comings and goings."

Utterson thought there must be dark secrets indeed between Mr Hyde
and Dr Jekyll; he didn't like the idea of that evil little rat of a man coming
and going furtively around the back of the doctor's house.

~3~
THE CAREW
MURDER CASE

Mr Utterson tried to talk to Dr Jekyll about Mr Hyde on several occasions, but the doctor just told him to let the matter drop. A year passed by, with Mr Utterson doing his best not to think about Mr Hyde at all. But then something terrible happened. One of Mr Utterson's clients was murdered, beaten to death in the street by a madman with a heavy walking stick. A woman who witnessed the attack said she recognised the murderer as Mr Hyde.

Mr Utterson went to the police and offered to show them where Mr Hyde lived. It was a foggy morning. The street lamps were still on, and the fog swirled around them, making clouds of orange light. Utterson took the police to Mr Hyde's house, and they knocked on the door.

A woman answered. She told them her employer, Mr Hyde, was not at home. She showed them his rooms, which were very untidy. There were clothes strewn on the floor, and drawers left open. There was a heap of grey ashes in the grate, including scraps of burned paper and the butt end of a green cheque book. Mr Hyde must have panicked because he seemed to have left in a great hurry.

Behind the door, they found a bloodstained walking stick. Mr Utterson recognised it as one he had given to Dr Jekyll several years before.

Mr Utterson went to see Dr Jekyll. Poole showed him in, and took him through the back garden into the laboratory, where the doctor had his private study. At the far end of the laboratory there were some stairs leading up to a red door. Poole knocked on the door and showed Utterson in. The study was a small room with three barred windows overlooking a courtyard. The doctor was sitting in front of the fire. He looked sick.

"Have you heard the news?" Utterson asked. The doctor nodded.

"Carew was a client of mine," said Utterson. "Your friend murdered him. Tell me you are not insane enough to be hiding him."

Dr Jekyll swore he would never see or speak to Mr Hyde again. He said he had received a letter from Hyde that very morning, and gave it to Utterson to read.

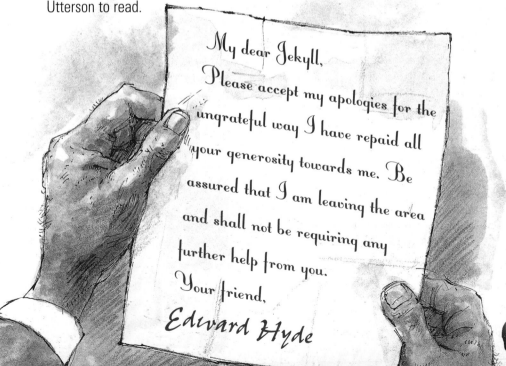

My dear Jekyll,
Please accept my apologies for the ungrateful way I have repaid all your generosity towards me. Be assured that I am leaving the area and shall not be requiring any further help from you.
Your friend,
Edward Hyde

Mr Utterson breathed a sigh of relief. It seemed that he had been wrong about Hyde blackmailing Dr Jekyll; the doctor had simply been helping him. But on his way out, Mr Utterson spoke to Poole. He asked what the messenger who brought the letter for Dr Jekyll that morning had looked like. Poole said there hadn't been any messengers to the house, or any post.

Mr Utterson was hurt and confused. Why should his old friend have lied to him? And how had he really come by the letter? As soon as he got home, he took the letter out of his pocket and read it again. There was something oddly familiar about the handwriting. Dr Jekyll's latest dinner invitation was still propped up on the mantelpiece, and Mr Utterson took it down. He laid it on the desk next to Hyde's letter. The handwriting was almost exactly the same, except that it was slanted differently.

Mr Utterson groaned. How could his dear friend Dr Jekyll have sunk so low as to forge a letter for a murderer?

My dear Jekyll,
Please accept my apologies for the ungrateful way I have repaid all your generosity towards me. Be assured that I am leaving the area and shall not be requiring any further help from you.
Your friend,
Edward Hyde

Dear Utterson,
I cordially invite you to a dinner party on Friday at 7.30pm
Your friend,
Jekyll

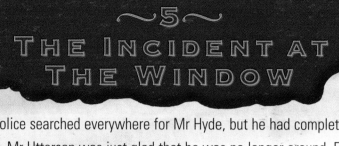

The police searched everywhere for Mr Hyde, but he had completely vanished. Mr Utterson was just glad that he was no longer around. For a while, Dr Jekyll became more like his old self again, more sociable and less secretive, and Utterson hoped they could put the past behind them.

But then one evening, Dr Jekyll refused to see him, and the same thing happened every night for the rest of the week. Mr Utterson wrote a letter to Dr Jekyll, asking why he kept instructing Poole not to let him in. Dr Jekyll replied immediately that he just needed to be on his own for a while.

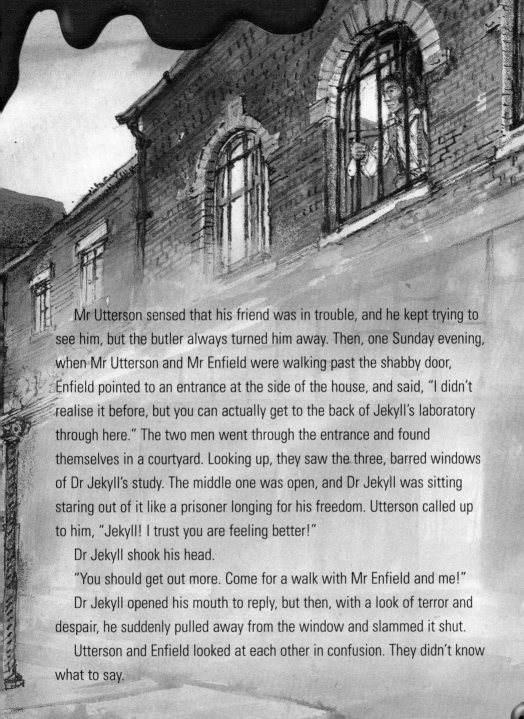

Mr Utterson sensed that his friend was in trouble, and he kept trying to see him, but the butler always turned him away. Then, one Sunday evening, when Mr Utterson and Mr Enfield were walking past the shabby door, Enfield pointed to an entrance at the side of the house, and said, "I didn't realise it before, but you can actually get to the back of Jekyll's laboratory through here." The two men went through the entrance and found themselves in a courtyard. Looking up, they saw the three, barred windows of Dr Jekyll's study. The middle one was open, and Dr Jekyll was sitting staring out of it like a prisoner longing for his freedom. Utterson called up to him, "Jekyll! I trust you are feeling better!"

Dr Jekyll shook his head.

"You should get out more. Come for a walk with Mr Enfield and me!"

Dr Jekyll opened his mouth to reply, but then, with a look of terror and despair, he suddenly pulled away from the window and slammed it shut.

Utterson and Enfield looked at each other in confusion. They didn't know what to say.

One evening in March, Mr Utterson received a visit from Poole. The butler seemed agitated. "Please come with me, sir," he said. "I think there has been foul play." Utterson followed him out into night, filled with feelings of foreboding.

When they got to Dr Jekyll's study, Poole knocked on the door. "Mr Utterson is here to see you, sir," he said. They heard a voice from inside say, "Tell him I cannot see anyone." Poole gave Utterson a meaningful look, and led him back down the stairs. "Was that Dr Jekyll's voice?" Utterson demanded. Poole was not sure. "Eight days ago we heard Dr Jekyll scream," Poole said. "No one has seen him since."

The servants were beginning to wonder if their master had been murdered. But why should the murderer lock himself up in the study? And why should he then behave so oddly? Night and day he had been calling out for medicine, and putting notes on the stair for the servants to take to the chemist. And every time they came back with what he had ordered it was the wrong thing, or not pure enough. Poole had one of these notes in his pocket, which he showed to Utterson.

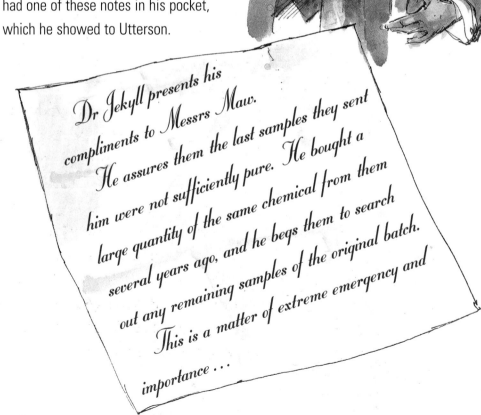

Dr Jekyll presents his compliments to Messrs Maw. He assures them the last samples they sent him were not sufficiently pure. He bought a large quantity of the same chemical from them several years ago, and he begs them to search out any remaining samples of the original batch. This is a matter of extreme emergency and importance . . .

Utterson said, "This is Jekyll's handwriting, Poole. What makes you think it isn't the doctor himself who is locked up in his study?" Poole frowned. He seemed to hesitate. "I have seen him!" he said at last. "I came into the laboratory and caught him rummaging through the packing crates. As soon as he saw me, he scuttled back into the study. If it was my master I saw, why did he have a mask over his face?"

"A mask?" said Utterson. "Why, man – it's all falling into place! Jekyll has locked himself up in his study because he has developed some hideous skin complaint. That's why he keeps sending for medicines. That's why he doesn't want us to see him!" Poole shook his head. "The man I saw was far too small to be Dr Jekyll ... Mr Utterson, I think it was Mr Hyde." Utterson gave a heavy sigh. "If that is what you think, then we have no choice," he said.

The two men armed themselves, Utterson with a poker and Poole with an axe. They went up the stairs to the red door. They could hear the sound of footsteps pacing up and down inside the study. Utterson knocked sharply on the door, and the pacing stopped.

"Jekyll!" he cried. "I demand to see you!"

There was not a sound.

"If you don't open the door," said Utterson, "we have the means to break it down."

Then a voice cried out, "Utterson! For God's sake, have mercy!"

Grimly, Utterson said, "That is not the doctor's voice. It is Hyde's. Break down the door!"

Poole struck the door with his axe. A piteous wail, like an animal in pain, came from inside the study. Poole hit the door again. Five times the axe struck the door before it finally gave way and the two men were able to go through.

They found Mr Hyde lying on the hearth rug, close to death, with a bottle of poison in his hand. "It is too late for him," said Utterson. "But where is Dr Jekyll?" There was no one else in the room. On the desk, there was a large envelope, addressed to Mr Utterson.

The envelope contained three items. The first was a new will, made out this time not to Mr Hyde, but to Gabriel John Utterson. The second was a note in the doctor's handwriting. It said, "When you read this, I shall have disappeared, although I don't know in what way. If you want to know more, you will find enclosed my final confession. From your friend, Henry Jekyll." The third item was Dr Jekyll's confession.

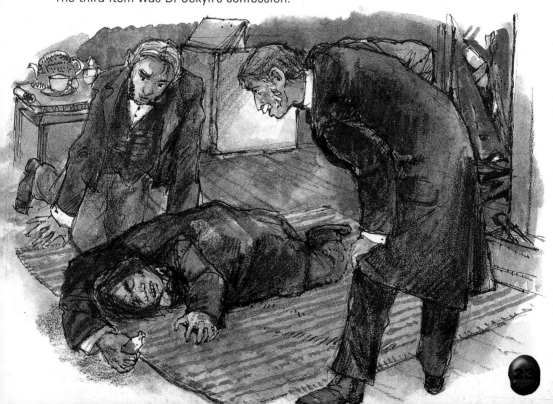

I was born into a very respectable family, and my ambition was to become a fine, upstanding member of society. I tried to devote myself completely to studying and helping other people. But there was also a part of me which only wanted to go out and have fun, and as this did not fit with my idea of how I should behave, I did my utmost to resist it. When the urge to go out on the town was too strong, I went secretly. In this way, I developed a double life.

I felt almost like two people living in the same body: a respectable doctor and a drunken reveller. I thought perhaps everybody had a split nature like me – one part that wanted to always do what was right, and the other that wanted to do whatever it liked. I started to fantasise about how it might be if we could actually separate the two. Then the moral side would be happy because it would be free from selfish temptations, and the immoral side would be happy because it would be free from guilt.

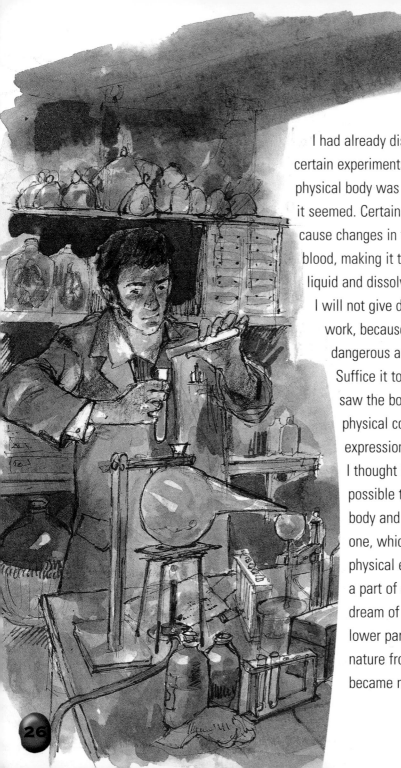

I had already discovered through certain experiments that the physical body was not as solid as it seemed. Certain chemicals could cause changes in the flesh and blood, making it tremble like a liquid and dissolve into a mist. I will not give details here of this work, because it is too dangerous and incomplete. Suffice it to say that as I now saw the body as merely the physical covering and expression of the soul, I thought it might be possible to dissolve one body and create a different one, which would be the physical expression of only a part of a man's soul. My dream of splitting off the lower part of a man's nature from the higher part became my scientific goal.

I hesitated for a long time before plucking up the courage to put my theory to the test because I knew it could result in my death. But finally I just had to find out if it would work. So I mixed the necessary chemicals and, trying not to think about the enormity of what I was doing, I drank the mixture down.

Almost immediately, I experienced dreadful pains throughout my body. I felt sick to my very bones. I was overcome by a surge of terror. Then as suddenly as it began, it was over. I seemed to recover. My body felt younger, lighter, happier; my mind was full of reckless thoughts, and I felt an overwhelming urge to do all kinds of wicked things. I had no conscience. I felt drunk with delight, but as soon as I moved, I realised that I was smaller in stature than before. This was probably because I had starved and controlled the evil side of my nature to such a degree that it was less well developed than the good side. I drank the potion again, to see if I could return to my former state. I suffered the same pangs of pain, and returned again to my original form.

I saw straight away that this power to have two separate identities could serve me well. I could be a respectable doctor, and at the same time lead a life of abandon and disrepute. I named my evil identity Mr Hyde, bought him a house, and engaged a housekeeper to look after it, knowing that Mr Hyde wouldn't be there all the time. I told my own servants that a Mr Hyde would be calling from time to time, and they should serve him if I was away. I wrote the will you objected to so much in case any mishap occurred and I could not return to the body of Dr Jekyll.

Now I could do whatever I liked in the form of Mr Hyde, not that I wanted to do anything really evil; I just wanted to have some fun. But as soon as I became Mr Hyde, he took over, and his desires were nothing short of monstrous. He delighted in hurting other people, and his heart was as hard as stone. Sometimes the things he did shocked me, but I told myself it was not me who had done the foul deeds, and I made up for it by working even harder at being good.

About two months before the murder of Sir Danvers Carew something very unsettling happened. I went to bed as Dr Jekyll, but when I awoke I was Mr Hyde! How had this come about? What if giving the darker side of my nature a free rein had made it grow more powerful? What if Mr Hyde were to take over completely? It was a moment of crisis. If I didn't choose one or the other, the choice might be out of my hands. I decided – as most people do – that I would prefer to try to be good. For two months I managed to live without Mr Hyde, but eventually it got too much for me, and I took another dose of the potion.

Having been shut out for so long, the evil spirit of Mr Hyde was more furious and hateful than ever. He went out into the darkness spoiling for a fight. Without the slightest provocation, he attacked Sir Danvers Carew and beat him to death. He felt nothing but fiendish delight. But no sooner was the man dead than Mr Hyde saw he was in deep trouble. He ran back to his house and burned his papers. He must go to ground! He must disappear immediately!

When I was back to my old form I had to face up to the horror of what I had done. I had unleashed a monster in creating Mr Hyde. I had committed dreadful deeds through him. He had gone too far this time, and I knew I must break free of him forever.

I threw myself into good works. I started feeling a little better about myself. One day I was sitting on a park bench and the thought came into my head that I probably wasn't any worse than other people; I might even be better, because I put so much energy into trying to do good. At that very moment a strange feeling came over me. I began to tremble. I felt sick and faint. When the faintness passed, I felt stronger, bolder, more reckless. I looked down. My clothes were too big for me. My hands, which are normally large and pale, had become small and sinewy, and covered in a mat of black hair. They were the hands of Mr Hyde!

I hurried home to get my drugs. I was desperate to be free of Mr Hyde but it was too late; the situation was out of my control. That afternoon, whilst walking through my garden, I felt the horrible changes coming over me and I had to run back to my study again. It took a double dose of the

potion to change me back to Dr Jekyll. After that, every time I fell asleep, I would wake up as Mr Hyde. Even dozing in my chair allowed the fiend to come. I dared not rest at all. Whenever I changed into Mr Hyde, I needed ever-increasing doses of potion to bring me back to Dr Jekyll again.

Then disaster struck! The chemical I had used for so long ran out. I sent for fresh stocks, but I could not get the potion to work. Later I discovered that the original chemical was impure, and it must have been the impurity that made the formula effective.

So you see, my days are numbered. I do not know how it will end, but I know that when the change occurs again, it will never be reversed. Whether Hyde will die on the scaffold or have the courage to take his own life in the end, I cannot say. It does not concern me. In a short time, Dr Jekyll will be no more. As for Mr Hyde, he is a different person.

Here ends the last confession and the unhappy life of your unfortunate friend, Henry Jekyll.